MW01129167

A portion of the proceeds from the sale of this book will
be donated to Australian Shepherd Rescue:

www.AussieRescue.org

Also by Devin O'Branagan:

Spirit Warriors

Witch Hunt

Glory

Red Hot Property

Red Hot Liberty

Show Dog Sings the Blues

Devin O'Branagan

Cornucopia Creations, Ltd.

Cover design by Laura Givens

This book is a work of fiction. Names, characters, places, and incidents are products of the author's imagination or are used fictitiously. Any resemblance to actual events or locales, or any person, living or dead, is entirely coincidental.

ISBN-13: 978-1461180913

ISBN-10: 1461180910

Published by:

Cornucopia Creations, Ltd.

This novel is dedicated to all herding/pastoral breeds of dogs. Whether we put them to work as stockdogs, or in trials, show, agility, dance, acting, sports, obedience, search & rescue, therapy, service, security, or as companions and best friends, their intelligence and courage is stunning. I am humbled by their noble spirits.

With this book, I especially want to honor the memories of my own late Australian Shepherds, Kolbe and Jazz. Forever, they will stay in my heart.

AUTHOR'S NOTE

Show Dog Sings the Blues is a spinoff from my comic novel, *Red Hot Liberty*, and expands an incident in that book from the dog's perspective. Talisman the Australian Shepherd is one of the most popular characters I have ever created, and this book finally allows fans to get inside her head and her heart. Well, actually, it allowed me to get inside her too, and that was a creative orgy full of delightful surprises. I have always loved Talisman but now admit to being deeply in love with her. She is an awesome Aussie.

Australian Shepherds were developed on ranches in the Western United States—despite their name, Aussies did not originate in Australia. They are valued by stockmen for their inherent versatility and trainability, and while they work as stockdogs and compete in stockdog trials, the breed has also earned recognition in every other imaginable canine role due to their eagerness to please. I can personally attest to the fact that they do not have a give-up-gene and are psychic. (Before I adopted my first Aussie, an old country vet warned me about their psychic ability, noting that it tended to frighten people.) Due to their independent spirit and high drive, Aussies are not for everyone. People considering adopting one should not proceed without fully investigating the special challenges they present. Unfortunately, too many end up with Aussie Rescue, at animal shelters, or worse.

I hope you will enjoy this glimpse into the delightful character of the Australian Shepherd.

CHAPTER ONE

My official name is Spiritsong's Lucky Talisman of DeMitri, but my friends call me Tali. I'm a pampered show dog, and even though I'm an Australian Shepherd I never expected to be standing over a baby lamb in a remote pasture, protecting her from two hungry coyotes. However, life is full of surprises, there are unfortunate incidents involving mud puddles, and if I survive this I promise I'll never make fun of my sister again for being a cowdog. It takes more courage than I ever imagined.

And more courage than I know if I have.

*   *   *

My sister Maddie was born adventurous. I was born beautiful. When Preacher Levi came to get a new puppy, I remember sitting there looking at him, batting my baby blue eyes. Meanwhile, Maddie climbed the gate of the kennel and jumped into his arms. The preacher, who owned a ranch in Colorado, liked Maddie's spunk and so took her home to Heavenly Acres Ranch where she grew up to be a cowdog.

Eventually, I found a person who appreciated my ability to be admired. His name was Valentino DeMitri, and he put me to work as a show dog. He taught me to stand square and still in what was called a stacked position so that show judges could examine me and see what a gorgeous Aussie I was. I had what was known as "perfect conformation"—my body conformed to the desirable standard of an Australian Shepherd. My blue merle coat was luxurious, and my sky blue eyes were surrounded by stunning black eyeliner that made their beauty just pop out. Because of all this, I won a lot of contests and became quite a legend in the show ring. Val was happy, and I enjoyed a life of luxury.

Then Val left this world, and I was adopted by a nine-year-old girl named Angelina who became equally devoted to me. Angelina and her mother, Molly, made sure I got massages by certified canine massage therapists, they took me to the pet psychic so I could communicate my wishes, and they manicured my nails, painting them a lovely shade of pink.

Val had left instructions for my care and feeding that included a calendar of regularly scheduled play dates with my sister, Maddie.

One Sunday in March, Angelina, Molly, and Molly's friend—a cowgirl named Jessie—finally took me to Heavenly Acres Ranch to spend the day with Maddie. I hadn't been there since Val's death. After dropping me off, they planned to accompany Preacher Levi to his church service.

As we all piled out of Molly's BMW, Preacher Levi was waiting for us and tipped his hat in greeting. "Ladies."

Jessie giggled. The entire trip here all she had done was gush about what a crush she had on the famous TV preacher, and now all she could do was giggle? Human mating rituals were a mystery to me.

Molly shook Levi's hand. "I'm Molly O'Malley and this is my daughter, Angelina." She gestured to Jessie.

"My friend, Jessie Dalton."

Jessie took his hand and performed an awkward curtsy, then giggled some more.

Levi didn't bat an eye—he was probably used to love-crazed cowgirls. "Nice to meet you, ma'am." He touched the brim of his hat and tipped his head.

Jessie practically swooned.

Levi knelt to greet Angelina and me.

"You're getting mud on your jeans," Angelina said to him.

"This is a ranch. I could be getting worse stuff on my jeans."

Angelina tossed her head and sniffed. "I guess that's true."

When Levi smiled at me his light was so bright that it warmed my heart, and I felt compelled to smile back. Shamelessly, I even kissed him. I understood why he made all the women melt.

"It's been a while, Miss Tali," he said. "We've missed you. I'm sorry for all your sorrow." He pulled my head into his chest, then bent and whispered, "Love is stronger than death. Ain't no force powerful enough to sever that special tie between you and Val."

His words touched my heart and I whined.

He kissed my ear, we smiled at each other again, and I felt more relaxed than I had in a long time.

Levi stood, whistled, and Maddie raced toward us from the barn, her ears laid flat against her head and her tongue flapping in the wind. She ran right up to me and we touched noses. Then she turned her back and gazed out at the vast realm that she ruled. Maddie liked to show off.

So I shook my head, which fluffed up the neck scarf I wore that said I'M QUEEN OF THE SHOW RING. I liked to toot my own horn too.

I had a tailless bottom that wiggled rather spectacularly when I was happy, but I was trying to contain my joy at seeing Maddie. I didn't want to seem overly excited because although I tried not to be judgmental, every time I saw her I was shocked by how, um, *earthy* she was. Like me, she had a blue merle coat—a marbled swirl of black and silver with copper highlights and white trim. However, her white was always gray with dirt, and her black and silver locks were often tangled. And, well, her nails were never, ever manicured. I tried to demonstrate my disapproval by not greeting her with a lot of hoopla. I sat down a respectable distance away and ignored her.

"Is Tali going to be okay?" Angelina asked. "She doesn't look very happy."

Levi smiled. "She'll be just fine. My new ranch hand here will make sure of it. Won't you, Josh?"

Josh was even dirtier than Maddie. He knocked the dust off his cowboy hat, spat some disgusting-smelling tobacco juice at the ground, and said, "Yep."

Levi performed introductions. "This is Josh and his wife, Cheyenne. They'll be in charge while everyone else heads into town for the service."

Molly nodded in greeting. "Please take care of Tali. She's...well, she's special."

"Yes, ma'am," Josh said.

"Remember that the two Aussie girls get to play for an hour, and then you put Tali in the house and let her relax for the rest of the day," Levi said. "She's a fancy beauty queen and is used to the easy life."

Cheyenne nodded. "I'll make sure she gets pampered right fine. She can keep me company inside while I do some chores."

"Then let's get on to the prayer meeting," Levi said. "After the service, there'll be a big barbeque. We won't be back 'til late."

Josh spat some more tobacco juice. "No worries. Cheyenne and me will hold down the fort."

Angelina handed my travel bag to Cheyenne. "This has her special treats, bottled water, and organic kibble. She eats three times a day. She's already had breakfast, but she'll need lunch before we get back. Oh, and be sure to give her one of the multiple vitamins with her food. And there's her plush throw to lie on. She just got groomed and doesn't like getting dirty."

Cheyenne's eyes grew wide, and she looked at me as if I were from Mars. "She is a dog, right?"

"A very pampered one," Levi said with a wink.

"Okey-dokey," Cheyenne said.

Angelina knelt and smothered me with kisses. "Have a good visit with your sister." She glanced at Maddie, who was still sitting with her back to me. "They do like each other, right?"

Levi chuckled. "They love each other. I've watched them play from the house. They get on fine when they think no one's looking. Trust me."

Angelina didn't seem at all convinced. "Maybe this isn't such a good idea."

Jessie threw Molly a panicked look. I sensed she was worried that the visit with her adored preacher was going to be called off, so I came to the rescue. I gave Angelina a kiss to say everything was okay.

"Y'all want to ride with me?" Levi asked.

Jessie beamed. "You betcha."

"Well, then let's git to gittin', 'cause the Lord's awaitin'."

I kissed Angelina again, hoping it would reassure her. I had been here many times before, and there was nothing for her to worry about.

My people left with Preacher Levi, Josh and Cheyenne wandered off to do chores, and Maddie and I ignored each other until we were alone. Then she turned around and sniffed me, so I stood and sniffed her too. For a time, it was a veritable sniff-fest. The smells on her fascinated me, much in the same way that the horror movies Angelina always watched never failed to suck me in. It was just so awful that it was hypnotizing.

I sensed Maddie's frustration at not finding many noteworthy scents on me. I had just been groomed, which limited the range of odors to those of the manmade, perfumed variety.

Finally, Maddie pulled back and grinned, which made my butt wiggle *spectacularly.*

Maddie crouched down in a play bow and gave me a happy yap. I met her bow before we both leapt up in a finely choreographed dance. We jumped high, twisted in mid air, and then came down at the same time. With a rush of shared delight, we slammed our butts together, and in a telepathic moment that rivaled any session with my private pet psychic, we chose that exact same moment to race away from the house toward a distant hilltop. It was glorious. This was always the best part of visiting Maddie—it was the only time I ever ran free.

We chased the wind. Exhilaration filled me as I ran. My perky ears lay back against my head, my pretty black lips were drawn wide in a smile, and my perfect pantaloons poofed out like flags behind me. The spring earth was soft and wet, and my toes gripped the ground, propelling me forward. I didn't even care that my beautiful pink nails were getting dirty. That's how much I loved to run with Maddie.

We came to the crest of the hill, skidded to a stop, and stood side-by-side panting and drinking in the amazing view. Heavenly Acres Ranch spread out below us as far as the eye could see. There were horses, cattle, sheep, geese, chickens, cats, and not another dog in sight. As much as I knew Maddie loved the prestige of being the only cowdog on this magnificent ranch, I also knew she was sometimes lonely for someone who spoke her own language. On some instinctive level Preacher Levi knew it too, which was why he encouraged my visits.

So, Maddie and I came to this hilltop where not another soul could hear us, and in our own special way we shared the news about our lives. I told her that Val had unexpectedly left this world, which was why Angelina and Molly had adopted me. I told her that sometimes I still saw Val's spirit, and he promised me he would be waiting at The Rainbow Bridge when my time came.

Val always had a special affinity for rainbows.

I admitted that I missed Val so much it felt as if my heart would burst with sorrow, but I was starting to love Angelina because she needed me. She was my job now.

Maddie told me that Levi needed her too, and that despite everything he had going on with God, he was lonely without a mate. She said that tending his heart was as important a job as tending his critters.

If people only knew that the destiny of dogs was much more significant than they ever imagined.

*   *   *

Now, I like cats. I really do. So I don't know what possessed me, but when the black and white one with the bushy tail skittered across the base of the hill below us, I was seized by an uncontrollable desire to chase it. I just couldn't help myself.

I charged down the hillside and Maddie followed close at my heels. However, it took me a moment to realize that she wasn't chasing the cat—she was trying to stop me, which made no sense until I caught the unexpected odor of skunk.

Uh, oh. As I tried to stop, I saw the frightened creature raise her tail. Then, mercifully, Maddie smashed into me and knocked me out of the line of fire. We both tumbled down the hill, landing in a tangled heap smack-dab in the middle of a deep mud puddle. Wet, disgusting goo soaked my coat all the way to my delicate skin—it was a well-groomed show dog's worst nightmare!

Actually, it could be worse, Maddie pointed out.

As the skunk's spray drifted in our direction, I had to admit she was right. Still, the mud all over me was totally gross. I crawled out of the puddle and found a nearby patch of damp grass where I sprawled and rolled. I snorted, snuffled, and squirmed, rubbing every inch of my body on the grass to try to wipe off the offending slime. Maddie sat down a few feet away, laughing at my frantic efforts. She didn't seem in the least bit bothered by her own icky condition.

I stood and shook, then dropped to the ground and squirmed some more. Tried as I might, it was useless. Where were your groomers when you really needed them? Cheyenne popped into my mind. I guessed she would at least give me a bath and rescue me from this awful predicament. Encouraged by the thought, I hightailed it back to the ranch house.

I raced as fast as I could, but the thick, sticky mess in my pantaloons seemed to slow me down. Just this morning they had been so lovely. Now, it felt like I was wearing a pair of those heavy leather chaps the cowboys wore. Ranch living certainly wasn't my style. Give me my pretty, pampered, perfectly poofed lifestyle anytime.

Maddie was right behind me. I glanced back at her and noticed she had my scarf in her mouth—it must have come off when I was slithering on the grass. As sisters went, Maddie was very thoughtful, but visiting her apparently involved far more danger than I bargained for. Perhaps this was something I should discuss in further detail with the pet psychic on my next visit.

The good news was that Cheyenne and Josh were waiting for us outside the ranch house. The bad news was that Cheyenne's scream was so high-pitched and shrill it actually caused me to yelp with pain.

"What have you two *done*?" Cheyenne sniffed the air. "You didn't get skunked, did you?"

I ran right up to her and sat obediently at her feet, waiting for the disgusting dilemma to be remedied. However, she looked past me at Maddie, who trotted up with my scarf still in her mouth.

Cheyenne snatched the scarf. "Like I don't already have enough work to do today. Come on Tali, let's get you prettied up again before they come to fetch you home." She grasped Maddie by the collar and started to drag her into the house.

Maddie and I shared panicked looks. I could tell that she was as horrified at the thought of being groomed as I was at the idea of not being groomed. Even with the mud, these humans should have been able to tell us apart.

I tried to follow Maddie, but Cheyenne pushed me away with her foot. "Get on, now. You've had your play time. We all need to do our chores."

No, no, no! I turned to Josh and raised my paw. Surely he would see the pink nail polish through the grime.

He furrowed his eyebrows and took my paw. "You gotta sticky-burr?" Carefully, he examined between my toes and pads and never even noticed Angelina's artistic masterpiece on my toenails. He let me go. "It's not there anymore, girl."

What was *wrong* with humans? Didn't they use their senses at all? How did they survive this long as a species?

I fought back my mounting fear. Certainly he could tell that my eyes were blue—Maddie had brown eyes. I batted them and gave him my most sincere look.

"You got something in your eye now?"

I batted my eyes faster.

He took a moment to look in each eye—each sky blue eye surrounded by stunning black eyeliner that made their beauty just pop out—and said, "Probably just some mud. I'll hose you down, and you'll feel better."

Hose me down? Gorgeous show dogs did *not* get hosed down. Show dogs were special. I posed in a classic stacked stance so he could see that I was a skilled show dog. As I stood square and still, watching him alertly, waiting for him to acknowledge my highly renowned conformation, he grabbed the hose and turned it on full blast.

Surely Josh was joshing.

When the blast of water hit me, some primal part of my brain took over and I howled. However, I wasn't howling for my wolfen ancestors. No. I was crying out to my show dog sisters for help: *Spiritsong's Sassyfras*

Sodapop, Spiritsong's Strawberry Sundae, Spiritsong's Sweet Sundrop, hear my plaintive plea! Send my groomers! Dispatch my handlers! Sassy, Berry, Sunny...rescue me!

I was a show dog singing the blues.

"Criminy, Maddie, what's your beef?"

Josh's callous disregard for my anguish startled me into silence.

I closed my eyes, held my breath, battened down my ears, and waited for the world to end.

The water assaulted me without mercy, but somehow I survived.

When he turned off the hose, I sidled up to him and shook the water off me as furiously as I could manage. There was a certain measure of satisfaction I received from getting him wet.

Unfortunately, Josh seemed unfazed by the shower.

"Okay, it's time to get to work. It's just you and me today, and we got more chores than a rattlesnake can shake its tail at."

Did he say rattlesnake? Worse, did he say work? What did he expect me to do, pose pretty for the cows?

"We gotta feed, vaccinate, move stock. Come on, girl." Josh headed toward a nearby barn.

I had no idea how to handle this situation. Panic-stricken, I looked at the house. Maddie was in the window, her eyes wide with alarm. She was standing on hind legs, her sweaty paws marking the glass with evidence of her own fear. My mind reached out to hers. *What do I do?*

Don't hurt my ranch, Maddie managed to communicate before Cheyenne grasped a handful of scruff and pulled her away from the window.

"Maddie!" Josh's voice was impatient. "We're already runnin' behind."

Reluctantly, I trotted off toward him. *God help us all*, I thought. *This isn't going to be pretty.*

CHAPTER TWO

Josh hooked a wagon full of hay bales to the tractor. "Okay, hop on." He climbed up into the tractor and jerked his head toward the wagon.

Excuse me? I was certain he couldn't mean for me to ride in the wagon, so I tried to figure out a way to climb up onto the tractor.

Josh watched my clumsy efforts with obvious confusion. "What in tarnation are you doin'?"

I sighed and sat down. I felt so overwhelmed that I actually whimpered. I hated crying in front of strangers. Val had always said that confidence was sexy, and I felt neither confident nor sexy.

Josh's hand slapped the steering wheel, and he jumped to the ground. As he stomped over to where I sat being all pitiful, I could smell his anger and tried not to cower too much when he approached.

He crouched down and his eyes seized mine. His voice was quiet. "Now, we're gonna get somethin' straight. This is my first day on the job, and they left me alone to do a lot of work that I can't do without you. Maybe what we have here is a communication problem, so I'm gonna let you know exactly what I want you to do, and you're gonna do it. *Or else.* Am I makin' myself clear?"

I laid my ears back on my head and averted my eyes.

"All right." He stood. "Get in the wagon and guard the hay so the cows don't pull any of the bales off. Now get to it."

He climbed back on the tractor, and I jumped into the wagon. Can you imagine? I had, after all, arrived at the ranch in an elegant BMW. I lay down as the wagon slowly headed toward the pasture.

I glanced at my foot and noticed that one of my pretty pink nails had already managed to chip. If I survived this day, my groomers would sure have a lot of repairs to make.

I was so distracted by the state of my pedicure that I didn't notice the cows until one stuck her face in mine. Her velvet brown eyes quickly assessed me and she knew I wasn't Maddie.

Only the humans were clueless.

The cow opened her mouth, took hold of a bale of hay, and pulled.

I stood up and batted her face with my paw.

Her eyes blinked, but she paused for only a moment.

No! I barked.

Josh glanced back at us. "Criminy, Maddie. Bite her."

Bite her? I didn't want to hurt anyone—I had a gentle heart.

The bale of hay teetered precariously on the edge.

"Maddie!"

His tone startled me, and I snapped at her nose.

Surprised by my bold behavior, she let go of the hay and stepped back.

I'm sorry, I told her, but she didn't offer me absolution. However, her expression did reflect a certain amount of respect that hadn't been there before. I stood a little taller and looked at the other cows who stared at me with curiosity. I snapped at the air just to show them I meant business.

I might have imagined it, but I got the distinct impression that they laughed at me.

Josh stopped in the middle of the pasture and called me down from my perch. He pulled a bunch of bales off the wagon, broke them up, and kicked to spread them around.

I was trying to avoid the messy mud puddles when I glanced up and saw an entire herd of baby calves charging toward us. It was terrifying! I froze, uncertain what to do, but all three of them flew right past me to one of the larger piles of hay, where they lay down and snuggled into the dry warmth of the fresh bed.

Relief flooded me. That sure was a close one.

"Smart little buggers," Josh said. "Even at a week old they know how to get dry and cozy." His attention was captured by a cow lying on the ground under one of the cottonwood trees. "Oh, looks like we gotta problem." With a sense of urgency, he headed toward her. "Come on, Maddie. I'm gonna need your help."

Oh, dear. I hoped it wasn't too serious a problem because I didn't know how much help I could possibly offer. I ran after him.

The herd was headed for the feed, so we moved around them toward the trees.

Josh's pace slowed as he approached the cow. "Don't want to spook you, sweetheart, but lemme see." His voice was quiet but not like it had been when he spoke to me. It was soft and soothing.

The cow looked at him, glanced at me, then her frightened eyes flew back to him. He knelt by her hind end where two tiny hooves were poking out. After examining her, he said, "The calf's stuck." He reached out and placed a gentle hand on the cow. "You're gonna let me help, sweetheart, 'cause we don't got no choice." His tone changed back to his uncompromising one. "Maddie, I'm gonna get her up, and we're gonna drive her back to the barn. She's not gonna want to go, so you need to round up some cows to go along as encouragement."

Sure. Okay. Um, how do I do that?

He glanced at me. "Move it, girl. We don't got no time to spare, or we'll lose them both."

Their lives depended on me? Oh, this wasn't good. I spun around and saw a familiar face. The cow I had bitten, Velvet Eyes, had followed us. I ran up to where she was standing with a young heifer and circled them a few times while trying to figure out how to make them move. Finally, I sat down in front of her and whined.

She blinked and stared at me with confusion.

"For crissakes, what are you doing?" Josh asked. He had gotten the cow on her feet and was steadying her. She seemed terribly weak.

We had to get this show on the road!

I thought of my Border Collie friend, Bippity Boppity Boo. Boo had the best eye in the business—she could control anything with her intense gaze, but I had no clue how to do that. What I did have going for me, though, was my psychic ability. Aussies were famous for being psychic, and I had inherited that trait. So, I stared into Velvet Eyes' eyes and tried to convey grave concern for the lives of Sweetheart and her baby. In my mind, I conjured a vivid image of Velvet Eyes and her heifer friend walking obediently with us to the barn. For good measure, I threw in the promise of some kind of special food treat. Surely there was something there they would like to eat that I could figure out a way to give them.

I finished up by sending these thoughts: *See, if you don't do this, they'll both die, and then Josh'll kill me, and basically there will end up being a whole lot of death going on. So, please ma'am, please help. If you do this, I promise to never bite you again.*

Velvet Eyes grunted, glanced at the heifer, and then stepped forward. The heifer followed her lead.

I sensed she was willing to help Sweetheart and eager for a treat, but mostly I think she just took pity on me for my pathetic ineptitude.

Of course, I could have merely been projecting my shame onto her.

Josh had Sweetheart alongside a fence. "We're gonna walk them along this fence line here right to the barn. You bring 'em on, girl, and keep 'em moving."

Sweetheart was walking slowly and trying to hang back. I barked at Velvet Eyes to urge her onwards.

I swear she rolled her eyes at me, but she trudged on. Soon, our little train was making slow, but steady, progress toward our goal. Velvet Eyes and the heifer were in front, Josh walked with Sweetheart, and I trotted alongside them.

Josh looked at me and shook his head. "You're a piss-poor cowdog, if I ever seen one. Why Levi keeps you around, I can't figure."

Even though I never claimed to be a cowdog, his words offended me. I mean, I was a stockdog by nature, but I needed a little time to figure out the technical details of the job.

I decided that since my natural inclination was to impress the alpha dog, I wanted to make Josh proud of me. But then again, I'd really rather just be safe and comfortable in the house.

I was not a dog who liked adventures.

*   *   *

Josh put Velvet Eyes and her companion in a pen and then disappeared with Sweetheart into the barn to pull the calf. He told me to "git," so it was a relief not to have any immediate duties.

I had promised Velvet Eyes some treats, and I was a dog of my word. I scouted around for food that might appeal to a cow, and my nose led me to a nearby bucket filled with small cubes of grain. Since the smell of cows covered the bucket, I presumed it was meant for them. I grasped the handle in my mouth and dragged it to the pen, under the fence, and then tipped it over so both the ladies could take advantage of my noble nature. As I turned to leave, Velvet Eyes uttered a soft moo. I presumed she was thanking me for being a bitch of substance.

Val had taught me well.

I didn't know how long pulling a calf would take but decided I should use my free time to figure out how to properly herd. I needed to find something to practice on and started to wander about the place. The first thing I noticed as my trek began was that there was poo everywhere. All kinds and shapes and colors and scents of poo. My nose told me it belonged to cows, horses, sheep, chickens, geese, dogs, cats, squirrels, rabbits, mice, and other animals I couldn't identify. Now, I came from a well potty-trained household, so I tried to avoid stepping in it as much as possible, but it was hopeless. In life there were natural kind of gals and supernatural kind of gals, and I definitely fell into the latter category.

As I was tiptoeing through the poo I spied a trio of geese, and my heart leapt with joy. Yes, my instincts told me that geese were herdable. The three were waddling around together, their rear ends fat and their postures tall and proud. I thought their feathers were lovely shades of brown. Excited, I ran right up to them, but they scattered, their wings flapping and voices honking with annoyance. Maybe I was a bit too enthusiastic. So, I retreated a fair distance and let them regroup.

I sat down right on the ground—so intent on my mission that I was suddenly oblivious to the dirt and muck—and planned my next move. The problem was that I was so full of anticipation I got hyper, which led to trembling and then, well, I lost my head and charged them again. This time the head goose wasn't such a good sport about it, and he got irritated with me. Actually, maybe irritated was too mild a word to describe his mood. When I descended on him, instead of running away, he ran toward me and bit my cheek!

I yelped, turned, and retreated, but Grouchy Gander chased me. His beak took aim at my butt, and he managed to deliver a few well-aimed pinches. Seemingly inspired by his bold and daring behavior, his female companions joined the chase, their wings flapping and their voices harsh and angry. They chased me right into a corner by a big pile of hay bales, where they proceeded to beat me up. I had been raised a lady, so I didn't fight back. Besides, Maddie had once told me that it was wrong to hurt the critters we were bred to work. Instead, I climbed up the steps of hay to the top of the stack where I licked my wounds and kept a safe distance until the victorious geese finished their gloating and wandered off to brag.

Herded by a flock of geese. I was totally mortified.

I lay down, rested my chin on my paws, and tried to stifle my whines. Life had been hard lately, and this was just the gravy on the meatloaf of my life. I closed my eyes and decided to go to my happy place.

I had once won Best in Show at Westminster. *Me.* Spiritsong's Lucky Talisman of DeMitri. I inspired, entertained, and was the best damn Australian Shepherd in the world at that moment. I did it for Val, and I did it for my breed. I was an awesome Aussie. I reminded myself I still was an awesome Aussie; I just had a learning curve to navigate.

Being a show dog had provided me many admirable qualities: discipline, spirit, charisma, and charm. Those in my profession were representatives of our breed, destined to pass on our special traits to future generations. I was proud of my accomplishments as a show dog, and I was determined to finish this day proud of my performance as a stockdog. It was in my genes and in my ancestral soul. I'd figure out a way to figure it out.

The sun was warm and I dozed—I dreamt of dancing with Val. He and I had a tradition of starting every single day performing our daily rousing celebratory tribal dance of success together. The ritual was designed to build our confidence and ready ourselves to face the day. We shook, shimmied, and pranced, and it really was rousing.

The dream image of dancing with Val shifted to dancing with Angelina. Angelina had already known a hard life, full of tragedy, and she needed all the celebratory confidence-building she could get. As I had told Maddie, Angelina was now my purpose in life. I needed to show her that she could rise above her circumstances and be more than she imagined. It was a lesson I hoped to help her mother learn too.

I dreamt that I was a show dog tragically mistaken for a cowdog, and I did such a heroic job that I inspired both Angelina and Molly. I had my very own ticker-tape parade down Main Street as a marching band played "We Are the Champions." People threw dog treats as I passed. It was glorious!

I woke up to find a tiny kitten nursing on my ear. It was a major letdown from the epic experience I had just been having.

I opened one eye and saw her clamped onto the tip of my ear, sucking away, purring her heart out, tiny paws enthusiastically kneading with eager hope of coaxing milk. Sky blue eyes the exact shade of mine looked at me adoringly. Her sweet-smelling fur had shades similar to my own hair—she could have been my daughter, if I had been a cat.

Geez, so what was I supposed to do now? I might be beautiful, but I wasn't heartless.

Before I could sort it all out, a really big Siamese cat leapt onto my bed, hissed at me, took a wicked slap at my nose with angry claws, grasped her baby by its scruff, and carried her away. Little Blue Eyes watched me all the way down the hay stack.

Ouch! My paw swiped the blood off my nose. This really was a dangerous place—the way things were going, I'd be lucky to get out alive.

Well, I certainly was wide awake now. I got up and stretched, then climbed down off my perch. Thirsty, I tried to figure out where to find a bottle of water. I had brought my own, but it was in the house. Perhaps Maddie had been able to explain things to Cheyenne, so I headed to check the situation out. I climbed up the porch steps and peered in the window.

Maddie was lying on the couch atop my super plush throw—she looked so clean. Was that a pink bow in her hair? It was the exact shade of pink as my nails and would have looked very nice on me. I raised my paw and tapped the window.

Maddie looked at me, leapt off the couch, and raced to the window. Her eyes were frantic. *Get me outta here!*

Let me in! I replied.

She stood up on her hind legs and started pawing at the glass as if she were trying to dig through it. So, I stood up on my hind legs and pawed right back at her. I really don't know what we hoped to accomplish, but desperation can cloud the mind.

"Stop that, Tali!" Cheyenne yelled. The cowgirl marched over to the window and gave me an irritated look. "Git, Maddie, you two had your fun. Go on now. It's time for Tali's lunch." She carried a bottle of my spring water in one hand and a bowl of my special kibble in the other—my organic turkey and sweet potato, apple, and cranberry kibble that Molly bought for me at The Back to Eden Tree Hugging Organic Granola Shoppe.

My stomach growled. I really wanted that kibble.

Cheyenne stuck the bottle of water under one arm so that she had a free hand with which to draw the drapes closed.

The nerve.

I had a bad feeling that Maddie was not normally fed lunch, so no one was going to care that I was hungry. And even though I knew this entire unfortunate state of affairs wasn't Angelina's or Molly's fault, I decided that I was going to give them the silent treatment when they came back for me. Even though I could be a reasonable dog, I was really peeved.

Deflated, I left the porch in search of water.

I noticed a wading pond for the geese and headed toward it, but Grouchy Gander saw me coming and ran me off. He was an evil little creature. So, I headed toward the pen where Velvet Eyes was, but the water tank was too high for me to reach. Earlier, I had seen a bucket of water in the barn and decided to give that a try. Unsure if I'd be welcome during a calf-pulling, I crept up to the barn and peeked in. The sight of the newborn calf thrilled me. The wet little calf crouched on a mound of straw, its mama hovering over it giving it a good licking. The calf bawled and struggled to stand. With ears laid back, it pushed itself up using its back legs and promptly fell face forward to the ground.

Mama continued to lick with a sense of urgency. It was important for that baby to stand and begin to nurse—the birth had been hard.

I looked at the calf's huge dark eyes and willed it to be strong.

The calf pushed itself up again and wobbled precariously. I resisted the urge to rush to its aid, but its mama took a step closer, and the baby braced itself up against her. With front feet spread wide for support, the little one defied gravity, weakness, and a fragile connection to this world to take its first trembling steps.

Josh stood a fair distance away with a smile on his face. "That's it baby," he said in the soft voice that was kind.

I caught my breath as it occurred to me that if it hadn't been for Josh and me, this moment would not have happened. It was heady stuff to realize how much of a difference one cowboy and his cowdog could make in the grand scheme of things. I was so overwhelmed that I grew dizzy and sat down with a thud.

Josh noticed me. "We did good, girl."

Yes, we did. I stood and quietly moved to his side.

Together, we watched as the calf latched on to a teat and began to suck.

"They're gonna be just fine now," Josh said. He reached down and patted my head. "Come on, we gotta lot of work to do."

I was so proud to walk out of that barn at his side.

We went to his pickup truck where he sat on the open tailgate, grabbed a canteen, popped off the lid, and guzzled. I looked at the canteen longingly and panted really hard for emphasis.

He noticed my attention. "Oh, your bucket's in the barn, ain't it? Best not go back in there right now." His chin jutted toward a nearby puddle.

Seriously? I sat down and gave him my best, *Harrumph.*

"Seriously?" he said.

At least we were on the same wavelength.

Josh sighed and shook his head. "Criminy. In all my years and all the outfits I've worked at, I ain't never seen a cowdog like you."

I continued to stare at his canteen and pant like a crazy dog. I added a classic whimpering whine for emphasis.

"Oh, for crissakes." He rummaged around in the bed of his truck, came up with a hub cap, slapped it against his leg to knock out the dust, and then poured water into it for me. He put it on the ground. "I'm thinkin' that you ain't really a cowdog, and the fellas just left you here with me today as a joke since I'm new and all. But I'll humor them. I guess they coulda left a rattlesnake in my saddlebag. That might have been worse."

Might have been worse? And what's with the rattlesnake talk again? A dusty old hubcap? Who was playing a joke on whom here? However, I was too thirsty to waste any time giving him lip, so I just focused on draining the bowl.

He rifled through a small cooler and pulled out a sandwich. My nose told me it was ham and cheese on sourdough bread with a hint of mustard. It smelled really good.

I tried my best theatrics on him again, but this time he just laughed at me.

After he had eaten every single delicious crumb of that sandwich *all by himself*, he stood, stretched, and called me to follow him. "I've got the yearlings to feed. I need you to keep them away from me while I fill the troughs." He chuckled. "As Cheyenne says, they're like an entire football team crowdin' in for a tapped keg."

Yearlings? I was guessing they were way bigger than the week-old calves who had frightened me so badly. Oh, this didn't sound like a good time. Sustenance would certainly have helped. I was getting more peevish by the moment.

Josh filled a wheelbarrow full of grain and rolled it into a pen filled with huge, hungry-looking beasts. Dismayed, I hung back and assessed the situation. The trough was in the middle of the pen, and as Josh headed toward it, they closed in on him.

I heard his quiet voice say in his uncompromising tone, "Maddie, cowdog up."

My adrenaline surged, the earlier incident with the geese flashed through my mind, and I knew just what I needed to do. I took a deep breath and charged the yearlings. The cattle scattered as the geese had done, and Josh had the space he needed to start filling that trough. However, I could see that I had to hold them back until he finished because that grain sure got them excited. I could feel their crazy grain-lust and grew worried for Josh's safety.

After the yearlings scattered, they regrouped in the corner. One really intense guy stepped forward, lowered his head, and seized my eyes with his.

This was not good at all. I knew that if I looked away, I was surrendering my power. I remembered something my mother had told us girls before we were taken from her. She gave a pep talk on the subject of confidence and one of the things she said was, *I want you to be tough bitches. You can't ever let others see your paws sweat, or you'll be flat on your back with your bellies exposed, having to grin submissively, and that's just not our family's style. Make me proud, girls.*

If I looked away from Mr. Intensity, he would see me as weak. So, I stared right back, lowered my head just like his, and did a slow walk toward him.

I'm out of my mind. He's going to kill me.

He snorted and pawed the ground with one foot.

I'm tougher than you, I said as I moved steadily forward.

Unimpressed, he took a step toward me. And then another. Behind him, his companions followed his lead and inched forward.

Within minutes, Mr. Intensity and I were practically nose to nose. He was not intimidated by my boldness.

My mind flashed to the look of respect Velvet Eyes had given me after I snapped at her nose, and I made the impulsive decision to do the same thing to this fella.

I bit him.

He blinked.

I did it again.

He looked away, and the yearlings behind him—

sensing the subtle shift in power—stopped their own slow push forward.

However, after a moment, grain-lust overcame Mr. Intensity's wavering will. He emitted a loud bawl, took a couple steps back and then charged forward, leaping right over me. I turned around, grabbed his tail in my mouth and hung on for dear life.

He dragged me a few feet, then whipped his tail all the way to the right, lifting me off the ground and swinging me around. I bit down harder, and he swung me around the other way.

Wow, this was embarrassing.

As the world grew dizzy, I noticed that I had managed to stop his advance, and the other cattle had scattered again. Then through the blood pounding in my ears, I heard Josh laughing.

Laughing? I was dying here!

"Come on, girl. We're done."

Oh, thank God. I let go and raced out of there as fast as I could run.

When Josh shut the gate behind us, he said, "You're real entertainin'."

Not exactly the effect I was aiming for, but at least he wasn't mad.

As we walked away, I smiled. *If my mother could see me now.*

CHAPTER THREE

Josh had a beautiful horse that he brought with him from his last home in Montana. She was black, and he called her Beauty, which wasn't all that original, but there was something to be said for the value of tradition.

He got chatty as he worked to trim her hooves. We were in one of the big barns, and I was glad to be able to lie down and rest my sore muscles after my adventure with Mr. Intensity. I was going to need a really good massage after today.

Josh put on some special chaps that held his farrier tools and went to work examining each hoof—cleaning, trimming, and rasping. I didn't think he would be doing any kind of painting of them when he was done, although I thought that with Beauty's coloring a bright, cherry red would be stunning.

"This is a nice outfit here from what I can tell," Josh said. "A real blessing to me and Cheyenne. After what happened, we had to get out of Montana. The pain was in the air we breathed there. We were smotherin'."

I wondered what had happened to him and his wife there. Whatever it was, the pain was huge because I could feel it flowing out of him like a cold, black wind.

He stopped working for a few minutes and stared off into the past. I wasn't sure what to do except be still and quiet. I was lying on my belly a few feet away with my chin resting on my front feet.

Few humans knew that dogs understood people way more than they could imagine. We noticed every single word of their body language, smelled every emotion, and most of us knew exactly what they were saying. Just because we couldn't respond with similar words, most humans considered us stupid and inferior. Except for the opposable thumb issue, we were quite an impressive species.

And, of course, some of us were more impressive than others.

While I was lying there pondering the amazing species that was canine, a feline invaded me. Much to my chagrin, I felt the little paws climb up onto my back, make the trek to my fluffy collar and settle down right between my shoulder blades. Soon, the tiny trespasser was kneading, purring, and totally embarrassing me.

My nose told me that it was Little Blue Eyes.

What was I supposed to do now? If I stood up, she would fall—I didn't want to hurt her. And she was so happy where she was.

I sighed.

Josh glanced over at us. "You gotta kitten on your back."

Tell me something I don't know.

His eyes darted beyond me. "Uh, oh."

I had a feeling as to what was coming.

Sure enough, Siamese Mommy stalked right up to my head, delivered two well-aimed blows to my ear, put her two front feet up onto my back, grabbed Little Blue Eyes by the scruff, and stormed off.

Owww! I rubbed the place on my ear where her claws had snagged, then licked the blood off my paw.

It was worth the pain and indignation to see Josh smile.

The event seemed to have snapped him out of his dark place.

"You're a *real* interestin' dog," he said.

Oh, you don't know the half of it. I could make you even happier if I could tell you about the time Val dressed me up as Xena: Warrior Princess for The Canine Costume Ball—I developed an interesting fan club as a result of that escapade. Then there's the fact I have a crush on Ellen DeGeneres and like to imagine I'm her when I dance—I wear a darling little vest and a scarf that says CALL ME ELLEN. *Then, of course, there are my many romantic misadventures full of forbidden love affairs and canine angst. People need entertainment to keep them away from the dark places, and I'm happy to oblige. Val was in show business and raised me to understand the value of it.*

Unfortunately, Josh didn't hear a word I said. He reached down to the floor, picked up a sizable slice of hoof, and threw it over to me. "Here's a snack, girl."

How insulting! I was a dog who ate organic kibble, not a dog who chowed down on dirty old horse hooves. I grimaced. I sniffed it. I turned up my lip in disgust. I touched it with my tongue. I nibbled on it. I liked it. I chewed it. I ate it. I hung my head in shame.

Later, I blamed the unfortunate incident on the fact that I had missed lunch.

After I had consumed every delicious morsel and licked the ground to be certain, I looked up and was startled to see Josh sitting on a bench staring at me. His expression was intense and his mood full of turbulent storm clouds.

Did I do something wrong?

"My boy would have liked you," he said. "Caleb asked

for a pup of his own, but we never got 'round to it. Then it was too late."

His raw pain slashed the air like lightning. I stood up and took a couple tentative steps in his direction. *What can I do to help?*

"He was fine one day, then the fever got hold of him." Josh's voice cracked. "Took over his brain and nothin' could stop the wildfire."

I moved closer. I wanted to protect him from the shadows.

"Caleb begged me to make the pain stop. Cheyenne begged me to save him. What kinda man can't protect his family?" Josh started to cry and I rushed to him, pressing the top of my head into his chest—I wanted him to know that my heart cared about his. He grasped hold of me, bowed his head, and shed his tears on me. I soaked them up and tried to absorb a measure of his pain.

"He had barely lived," Josh managed to say. "Now he's gone. Why?"

I had a lot of experience with death. Both of the people in my last pack had died. Both had been taken violently and unexpectedly, and I knew the pain of loss. Those tragedies had taught me some powerful lessons. It seemed to me that the great mystery wasn't why someone died, but why that person had been here at all. Life was the miracle, and love was the reason for that miracle. I wanted to tell him that the pain would someday get better and what would remain was the beauty of that special person. Most of all, I wanted to say that love really was stronger than death. But I couldn't say those things. Instead, I pressed myself into his heart even harder and let him grieve, so he didn't have to face it alone. I suspected that he was the type of man who couldn't easily show his sorrow, especially around those who needed his strength. I would hold his pain and keep his secrets. That's the kind of dog I was.

*   *   *

An hour later, Josh's thunderstorm had passed—although dark clouds still lingered—and we headed out toward a distant pasture. Josh rode Beauty, and I trotted along at their side. Josh had grown quiet, so he hadn't yet told me what our next mission was. I hoped it wouldn't be something too challenging because I was really tired. Normally, my days were spent getting a whole lot of beauty sleep.

The day had warmed up, and a gentle breeze carried new and exotic smells. I thought about my life and how I spent most of it indoors with Molly at her office, comfortably ensconced on the couch at home, or sleeping with Angelina in her bed. I was a lucky dog and enjoyed my life of luxury, but there was something to be said for performing a hard day's work in the great outdoors.

Of course, I wouldn't want to do it again.

My nose picked up the strong scent of cattle. It was much more pungent than any animal smell I had yet encountered.

"We're gonna move the bulls to the next pasture over," Josh said.

Bulls? A whine escaped me.

He grinned. "Exciting, ain't it?"

Josh and I had very different ideas about what constituted a good time.

We reached the rise of a low hill and looked down at the pasture below—and there they were. A sea of bulls.

Omigod, it was like the seventh circle of bovine hell.

Josh pointed to a big gate on the far side of the pasture. "I'm gonna open that gate, and we're gonna move them to that pasture yonder."

Sure we are.

"What a good-looking herd," Josh said as we headed down the hill toward the pasture. "The bigger ones look to be around a ton." His grin widened. "I love a challenge."

Oh, for crissakes. I wondered who had more testosterone, him or them. What was it with men?

On that subject, I was well-known in my own circle of friends for being a tad gender-confused. I was famous for raising my leg like a boy dog in order to make personal statements. This seemed like an ideal time to make one of those, so right before he opened the gate to the pasture I paused at one of the posts, raised my leg, and peed all over it.

Josh chuckled. "Feeling tough, are you, girl?"

Nope. Not me. Just putting on a show. I'm good at that.

He jumped down and unhooked the gate, led me and Beauty inside, and closed it. He climbed back onto Beauty, smiled, and said, "Well, cowdog it up good. This ain't no time for slackin'. You push 'em, and I'll funnel 'em through the gate on the other side." With that, he kicked Beauty into motion and rode around the small herd to open the gate on the other side.

I watched as he got the gate open and gave me a signal that I supposed meant to "push 'em."

I can honestly say that never in my entire life had I ever been more terrified. This was a nightmare beyond comprehension. When the ginormous, mean-smelling monsters took notice of me, any confidence I had managed to muster during my adventures of the day dissolved in an instant. So, I decided to do what I always did to bolster my confidence—I did my daily rousing celebratory tribal dance of success. I crouched in a play bow, then leapt into the air where I spun around and landed facing the opposite direction. Falling to the ground, I rolled completely over and bounced to my feet, facing back the other way. I kicked each foot in turn, in sync with the music in my mind, and pranced about in a circle while imagining the theme song to the movie *Fame*. The song, "I'm Gonna Live Forever," seemed especially inspiring—and hopeful—given the circumstances. Since the music was just in my head, I thought a little singing wouldn't hurt. Inside I was singing, *I'm Gonna Live Forever*, but it came out as melodic barks punctuated by wild howling. That was okay because it was the thought that counted—and right now living forever was a really important thought.

I was so caught up in my dance that I didn't immediately notice the stampede.

Oops.

I didn't think this was exactly what Josh meant when he told me to "push 'em," but at least they were going the right direction, so I took off after them. Over the chaos, I heard Josh yelling and cursing. When the dust finally cleared, I saw that all the bulls had successfully gone through the gate and were in the correct pasture. However, to my horror, I saw Josh on his knees next to the closed gate, leaning forward and looking like he was about to collapse.

Oh, no! What had I done? I was a bad bad cowdog. Panic seized me, and I charged to his side. When I came up to him, I was stunned to see him laughing. No, not just laughing, but laughing *hysterically*. Seeing me, he shook his head. When he could finally talk, he said, "You're just one plum loco dog. Ain't never seen anythin' like you in all my born days." He grabbed me in a bear hug and flipped over onto his back, taking me with him. For a few unladylike moments, I was lying on top of him with my feet straight up in the air. Then he kissed the top of my head, released me so I could regain a more dignified pose, and said, "Darlin', you're one of a kind."

Well, he called me "darlin'" instead of "girl," so I figured that was a good sign. Maybe he wasn't going to kill me after all.

He laughed some more. Finally, he was laughed out, and we lay there together in silence. He stared at the sky, while I rested my chin on his chest and stared at him. His dark clouds were all gone now. One of his hands found my ear and rubbed it with gentle fingers. "Can you feel the heartbeat of the earth?"

I always feel the heartbeat of the earth.

"Life goes on, don't it?"

Yes, it does.

"Thank you for today, darlin'."

You're welcome. Glad I could help.

*   *   *

Josh had to get vaccinations ready to give the sheep, so he said I could have some time to myself. It sure had been an eventful day, but my instincts told me it was only around mid-afternoon. I wondered how much longer it would be before Angelina and Molly returned. I really wanted to go home.

With everything that had happened, Josh forgot to get the bucket of water out of the barn for me. I thought maybe Sweetheart and her baby might have settled down enough by now to not be spooked if I crept in there and got a drink.

The door was slightly ajar, so I pushed it open enough to squeeze through. Sweetheart and her calf were lying all snuggled up together on a clean pile of hay in a far corner. Slowly, so as not to seem threatening, I went to the bucket and practically drank it dry. Then I sat down and watched them for a few minutes. The baby looked at me with its giant eyes, and I gave it a silent blessing for a good life. Sweetheart seemed to sense my intent and wasn't bothered by my presence. After a while, I went outside and headed over to check on Velvet Eyes. She saw me coming and walked to the gate of the pen to greet me. I think she probably wanted some more treats, but she might have just wanted to say hi—I really am a likeable dog when I'm not biting noses. I was grateful to her for how she had helped us today, so when she bent low, I stuck my tongue through the gate and licked her nose. Then I saw Little Blue Eyes. She had run over to see me, overshot her landing site, and ended up in the pen precariously close to Velvet Eyes' hooves. Alarmed, I dove under the fence, grasped her by the scruff of her neck, and yanked her back out.

She uttered a tiny, little mew but didn't struggle. What was wrong with her mother, letting her run wild at this age? This was a dangerous place. My temper flared. I turned around and spotted Siamese Mommy headed my way, her mood as annoyed as mine. I marched right up to her and deposited Little Blue Eyes at her feet. She narrowed her eyes and raised her paw to slap me, but I met her with an expression that screamed, *Don't even think about it!*

Wisely, she thought better of it, lowered her paw, grunted, picked up her baby, and stormed off in a huff. Little Blue Eyes watched me adoringly until she was out of sight. I sent her silent blessings for a good life and hoped she would be safe without me. I'd have to ask Maddie to keep a special eye on her.

I decided to try to take a nap and headed over to my hay stack to catch a few winks. On the way, Grouchy Gander saw me and charged, but this time I wasn't going to take any guff. I lowered my head, set my sights on him, and slowly walked in his direction. For a moment it looked as if it might be a fatal case of chicken, but he veered out of my path, and with a great flurry of honking and flapping wings, retreated to the safety of his flock.

That's better, I said. *Glad we finally got that straight.*

Slowly, I climbed to the top of the hay pile where I had taken my earlier nap, curled up in the sun, and fell asleep.

People often spoke about their "heart dogs," the special ones that they love more than all the rest. Well, Val was my "heart person." I would never love another in the special way I loved him. He was always in my dreams, and he came to me then, dressed in his dapper tuxedo and top hat. His favorite song was "Say a Little Prayer," and that music played while we danced together. Afterward, I said to him, *Forever, you will stay in my heart.*

He smiled that brilliant smile of his that was like the sun itself. "I am so proud of you, my sweet Tali."

Whatever else happened, that was all I needed.

CHAPTER FOUR

Josh, Beauty, and I headed out to the pasture where the sheep were kept. Josh wanted me to help move them to one of the pens where he had set up a chute. He told me I would have to push them through the chute so he could give them their vaccinations. After everything else that I had been expected to do, it seemed pretty simple to me, which was a good thing because I was still so tired. Despite my catnap, Josh had to work hard to get me moving. And I was really sore—this just wasn't my usual gig. However, the day was almost over, and I was eager for a bath, dinner, extra special treats, and a really long, sound sleep. Then there would be a massage and a visit with my Reiki Master to help rebalance my aura and energy field—this had been a traumatic experience. Of course, I would have to tell everything to my pet psychic so he could let Angelina and Molly know just how mad I was at them about it all. I was not a dog who sugar-coated her feelings.

We made it to the sheep pasture and there they were— about thirty sheep and lambs standing together as if they'd been waiting for us.

"Well, after I've seen how you cowdog, can't wait to see how you sheepdog," Josh said.

I had never been around sheep before, and when I moved in to them I got really excited. Actually, I was practically giddy. I mean I was a shepherd, but my reaction did take me by surprise. It was like the time Molly had a visitor who wore a sheepskin coat—I got real excited then too.

The sheep were closer to my size than the cows had been, and I wasn't at all frightened of them. Oh, and their smell was heavenly. I longed to run up to them to sniff, snuffle, and generally fill myself to the brim with their essence, but they knew I wasn't their usual dog and seemed wary. So, I ran around the perimeter of the flock and inhaled the ground where they had been. I found an area that was well-coated with their poo and—God help me—I fell to the ground and rolled around it. I grew intoxicated. It was glorious!

"You okay, darlin'?" Josh asked.

Oh, I'm better than okay. This is thrilling!

However, I quickly realized my exuberance was making the sheep nervous—just like it had made the lady in the sheepskin coat nervous—so I struggled to get a grip on my emotions.

"If you're done bein' downright silly, bring 'em on. We got work to do."

Sure, no problem. I know just what to do. Don't know how I do, but I do!

I circled behind and got them moving. The flock seemed accustomed to being worked by a dog—Maddie had trained them well. They obediently grouped up and moved steadily forward, following Josh and Beauty. I kept running half-circles around the back of the flock to keep them all together. This was the most fun I'd had all day!

While I was running back and forth, I happened to glance back, and that's when I saw her. A tiny little lamb was lying on the ground against the back fence. *Oh, no!* I left my position and raced to her. She was really young—just a day or two old—but she didn't seem hurt. I nosed her thoroughly, and she didn't smell sick. I couldn't find anything to account for her being on the ground, except I sensed she was more weak and frail than she should have been. I tried to urge her to stand but she wouldn't—or couldn't. I wasn't sure what to do because Josh was too far away to hear my bark. I needed to race ahead and convince him there was an emergency. This was one of those moments in life when my theatrical training would definitely come in handy.

I'm not abandoning you, I assured Baby Lamb. *I'll be right back.*

Her expression was trusting.

I was just about to leave when I noticed two coyotes crouched low in the grass about twenty feet away.

My adrenaline surged and my hackles rose. I scanned the pasture looking for other coyotes. My eyes flew to my flock to make sure that none had strayed away from the group. Then I made the most important decision I had ever made in my life.

I decided to stay with my lamb.

Slowly, I moved to stand over Baby Lamb. I sensed her relief at my presence—after my roll in the poo, she likely found my sheep smell strong and comforting.

I'll protect you, I promised her. I wasn't exactly sure how I would do that, but I was going to give it my best shot. Of course, keeping her alive meant being able to keep myself alive, and I didn't know how I was going to do that either. There were two of them and only one of me. They made their living by hunting and killing. I made mine by looking pretty.

I thought of a lot of colorful swear words at that

moment but didn't want to upset my charge more than she already was. Instinctively, I knew that being mad was a better survival technique than being scared, but as the two coyotes stood and slowly advanced on us I felt a terror that was beyond even what the bulls had inspired. What was I supposed to do? I was beautiful, not strong. My legs felt like they were going to give out. A whimper escaped me. I fought the urge to run.

"You're much more than just a pretty face," Val said.

Startled, I jumped at the sound of his voice. I looked up and there he was, standing over me.

He smiled. "Believe in yourself, Tali."

What do I do? I asked.

"Just like in the beauty pageants—keep your eye on the prize. Do whatever it takes to win."

I had always been a fierce competitor, and I never let the competition intimidate me.

"I believe in you. You can do this," he said before fading away.

I can do this. I will be victorious.

The coyotes were a male and a female. They were about my size, but I looked a lot bigger because—being a show dog—my fur was long, thick, and luxurious. And right now, with my hackles raised, I looked impressive.

The coyotes held their fluffed up tails straight back to display aggression. Since I didn't have a tail, I couldn't mirror their signals. However, I did lift my ears high and push them forward, then bare my teeth. Intimidation was the name of the game at this particular moment.

I had a beautiful singing voice, and great command of it, so I decided to sing an opera and hit those bass notes with power. I barked like I had never barked before, making my voice sound deep and dangerous. Yes, I was the devil in the opera *Faust*, and the coyotes had better run, not just for their lives, but for their souls as well because I was a force to be feared.

They felt my power and backed off.

I paused to catch my breath and comfort the baby that was now shivering beneath me. If she had been stronger, she would have bolted. Bending down, I nuzzled her and tried to explain that I was not the enemy. The barriers between our minds fell away. I saw that the reason she was so weak was because she was one of a set of twins, and her mother had rejected her. Sadness filled me, fueling my desire to save her.

It didn't take long for the coyotes to return. This time they split up as they descended on us, one from the right and one from the left.

I invoked my inner guard dog, summoning her with a visceral growl from the core of my being. The growl grew like the thunderous approach of monsters from hell, and when the female coyote was close enough, the demons in me charged and drove her back. Then I spun around and charged the male—wicked teeth leading my attack. This time I didn't deliver a gentle nip on the nose but a full-on bite that drew squeals and blood. Startled, he retreated to his mate.

Leaping back to Baby Lamb, I resumed my sentry position.

I licked the blood off my lips and swallowed my victory. My heart pounded, my body trembled, and I braced myself for the next round. How long could I keep this up?

Val had been fond of telling me that Australian Shepherds didn't have a give-up-gene. I reminded myself that I had once been the best damn Aussie in the world.

Then I heard the sound that made my blood run cold. The coyote couple did a call out for their pack—their howls summoning the reinforcements that would help them kill Baby Lamb and me. I was overcome by a desire to run away.

Val, I need you.

He returned. "I'm here."

Tell me what to do. If I leave now, I'll be okay. If I don't, we'll both die.

"Death isn't the worst thing. Could you live knowing you abandoned her to die alone?"

I thought about it. *Does it hurt to die?*

"Nature helps. She's more merciful than she seems."

Will you stay with me when the time comes?

"I'll never leave you. I love you."

I love you too, Val. Forever and ever. You're my heart person.

I heard the yips, barks, and yowls that were the pack's answering call. It was on its way.

Val had spent his life on a spiritual journey, and he took me along for the ride. He spent countless hours God-bathing, which was how he described contemplation. I, on the other hand, sun-bathed—it required much less effort. Twice a day at certain times, Val went to his private chapel, chanted his sacred word, and disappeared into some inner space that provided him comfort. I randomly relaxed in the sun. On cloudy days, I still derived comfort from my ritual because I knew the sun was always there whether I could see it or not.

Val developed his spiritual system by studying the great mystics of all ages and distilling their wisdom. I developed mine by smelling things. My nose taught me that everything was unique. No two people, two animals, two plants, or even rocks smelled the same. Did all that uniqueness come from something or nothing? The answer was obvious to me.

I leaned down and smelled Baby Lamb, then I closed my eyes and felt the sun. That was my prayer. That was my hope.

*   *   *

The coyotes came. I felt their approach and braced myself, determined to go out with a mighty fight. I was an awesome Australian Shepherd.

I decided to greet them with a song, and "I'm Gonna Live Forever" seemed the appropriate choice. My melodic barks and passionate howls carried in the wind. Despite what was coming, I was filled with a feeling of joy which I hoped would touch Baby Lamb and give her comfort.

The pack came over the rise and headed toward us. I lifted my hackles, bared my teeth, and gathered every ounce of courage I had.

As I watched, the coyotes came to a halt, turned tail, and ran. Through the thunder of my blood, I heard Beauty's approach, Josh's shouts, and a gunshot pierce the air. Josh and Beauty galloped toward the pack and ran it off, then turned and raced to us. Josh jumped down and crouched in front of me.

"You okay, darlin'?"

I was trembling so hard I could barely stand.

He examined where the coyote's blood had stained my face, put his arms around me, and drew me close. "It's okay now. You did real good."

My heart leapt. I had finally made him proud of me.

When my trembling stilled, he picked up Baby Lamb,

mounted Beauty, and called me in his soft voice that was kind. "Let's go home, darlin' girl."

*   *   *

Josh rode to the preacher's house, sat on his horse, and called for his wife to come outside.

I experienced a moment of hope that Maddie would manage to rush the door when Cheyenne opened it, but she couldn't get past the wily cowgirl.

Cheyenne came out to us.

"I've got a lamb that needs tendin'." Josh said. "Can you come to the barn and take care of it while I go pen the sheep?"

Cheyenne reached up to Josh's lap and stroked Baby Lamb. "Sure, honey. What happened?"

"I don't know why this one's mama left her behind, but I reckon she's in need of some bottle-feedin'," Josh said. "Maddie here fought off some coyotes who wanted lamb steak for dinner."

Cheyenne noticed the blood on my face and knelt to get a better look. "Is she hurt?"

"Naw, that's coyote blood. When she left the flock, I was so mad at her for slackin' off that I was going to give her a real personal piece of my mind. Never expected what I found. This here is a good dog."

Yes, I am.

Cheyenne stroked my cheek. "Well, I'll clean her up a bit and meet you at the barn."

Josh nodded. "I was gonna give the flock their shots, but that can wait a while. I reckon Maddie needs a break. I'll just put them in a holding pen 'til later."

"Be there in a few," Cheyenne said.

Josh rode off, and Cheyenne ducked back in the house, returning a few minutes later with a pan of warm, soapy water and a wash cloth. She cursed as she negotiated the front door, and her foot pushed Maddie back. Then she came over to me, knelt, and washed away the blood. "That sister of yours is ornery beyond belief. Nothing I do seems to please her. She hated her bath, won't eat her food, and spent the entire day staring out the window whining her heart out."

I glanced at the window and saw Maddie. Nope she didn't look in the least bit happy—but she sure looked clean. I, on the other hand, was gross beyond belief, and just wiping coyote blood off my cheek wasn't going to help at all. However, Cheyenne stood up and smiled at her accomplishment. "There you are Maddie, looking all clean and pretty."

She sure had a strange sense of humor.

"Well, I gotta go feed that little lamb, so you rest for a bit. Then you can help Josh finish up with the sheep."

Good grief—they thought just a little rest would make up for the trauma of a near-death experience? They planned to send me right back to work? Unbelievable. And Maddie liked this life? Did we actually come from the same womb?

Well, it looked like Maddie was going to be able to work the sheep after all because I suddenly sensed that Angelina and Molly were almost here, and this nightmare was about to be over.

Cheyenne set the pan down on the porch, got into her pickup truck, and headed toward the big barn to meet up with Josh.

Me? I just sat there waiting for rescue. While waiting, I pushed back my mounting excitement at being reunited with my pack because I didn't want to seem happy. No, they had to know just how much I had suffered today. I was on a righteous mission to punish everyone involved for allowing this tragic situation to unfold.

So, I sat in the driveway in front of the house, practicing looking pitiful, and waited for Preacher Levi's truck to pull up with my people on board.

And there it is! It's turning in the drive now!

I reminded myself how cruelly I'd been treated.

I'm going to see my people!

They should have dressed me in my Ellen DeGeneres vest so I was easily identifiable.

Oh, there's Angelina! I love her so much!

But if I seemed too happy they might not exercise the proper amount of caution next time.

Angelina jumped out of the truck calling my name. When she saw me, she screamed, rushed over, knelt in the mud, and threw her arms around me.

Angelina is hugging me! She's so sweet!

I worked mightily to rein in my excitement.

Molly, Levi, and Jessie scrambled to us.

"What did they do to you, Tali?" Angelina's voice was tremulous. "Oh, my poor sweet Tali, whatever did they *do?*"

I sat rigidly, staring straight ahead, not making eye contact, and trying not to look as happy as I felt.

"Is she hurt?" Molly crouched and frantically patted me down.

Oh, their touch feels so good. I need to get away from it or I'll break out in song. I stood and wiggled out of their grasp, moved two feet away, and sat down again. I leveled them both with my most reproachful glare.

"She looks really pissed off," Jessie said.

Josh and Cheyenne's pickup truck rumbled toward us, parked, and they jumped out. "We heard a scream," Josh said.

Angelina stood and pointed at me with one hand and them with the other. "*What* did you *do* to my dog?"

The couple appeared confused.

"What are you talking about? Tali's in the house all safe and sound like I promised," Cheyenne said. She climbed the porch stairs, opened the door, and looked inside. "Come on, girl, your folks are here for you."

There was no movement from the house.

Cheyenne's voice turned impatient. "Well, come on, Tali."

Very slowly, almost reluctantly, Maddie walked out onto the porch, the pretty pink bow tied to a curly lock of hair atop her head. She sat down at the top of the stairs and gave everyone the evil eye.

"She looks really pissed too," Jessie said.

"Why should she?" Cheyenne asked. "I pampered her right good today."

Angelina's hand trembled as she pointed at Maddie. "*That's* Maddie." Her finger jabbed toward me. "*This* is Tali."

"Whoops," Cheyenne said.

"Oh, Lord," Levi said.

Josh frowned. "Well, that sure as hell explains a lot." A tentative grin played at his lips and he looked at the preacher. "I just thought you had the worst cowdog this side of The Rocky Mountains."

Did he actually call me the worst cowdog this side of The Rocky Mountains?

"You made Tali work cattle?" Levi asked.

Josh grinned. "Well, she didn't exactly work them.

More like she caused a bit of a stampede."

"Stampede?" Levi asked.

"Well, the dog kinda spooked them. See, the bulls scared her, she did this crazy little dance, and, well, we had a bit of a situation. But it worked out okay."

Molly used a cough to hide her smile.

Angelina was indignant. "Tali is a *show* dog, not a *cow* dog."

Josh's grin widened. "So, that's why she kept posing for me. And why she didn't want to drink puddle water. And why she howled when I hosed her down."

"You turned a *hose* on her? Show dogs do *not* get hosed down." Angelina was beside herself.

Jessie made a valiant effort to hide her bubbling laughter.

"Didn't you notice her blue eyes and her pink toenails?" Angelina asked.

Josh took off his hat and scratched his head. "Well, no, but she did keep battin' her eyes at me and raising her paw. Maybe she was trying to show me. I just thought she had something stuck in them."

Laughter burst from Jessie like water gushing from a hose.

"It's *not* funny," Angelina insisted.

Jessie fought to catch her breath. "Yeah, honey, I'm afraid it is."

Angelina stamped her foot. "What about Tali's QUEEN OF THE SHOW RING scarf? That should have been a clue."

Cheyenne pointed at Maddie. "When they came back from playing, both were real muddy, and she had the scarf in her mouth."

They all stared at Maddie.

Cheyenne giggled. "Hell, that would explain why she

didn't want to be groomed. And why she kept pawing at the inside of the windows all afternoon. She was so nervous that her paws got sweaty and left streaks— must've been scared about what her city sister was doing to her ranch."

Levi moved to pluck the pink bow from Maddie's hair. "I'm sorry girl. I bet you're a mite humiliated by all this." Despite his comforting words, he chuckled.

Maddie tossed her head and issued a loud sigh.

So, I tossed my head in exactly the same manner and echoed Maddie's sigh with perfection. We were both proud queens who had been dethroned, and our indignation was as thick as the mud that coated me.

Molly erupted in a belly laugh that had a ripple effect, and soon all of the adult people were in hysterics.

I looked at Maddie and she looked at me. At the exact same moment we decided to take off together at a hard run, our ears laid back, our direction toward the top of a distant hill.

I heard Angelina scream at the adults for making fun of us, and I was proud. I *really* did love her. However, at that moment, I wanted to be with Maddie more than anyone else. She was my sister, and I really loved her too. Today had been a milestone in our relationship, and we had a lot to share.

All my fatigue melted away as we ran together to our special hilltop. Joy filled me. I had survived, and behaved nobly, and was safely reunited with my pack. What more could any dog hope for?

When we came to rest at the top of the hill, Maddie rolled around in the dirt to get rid of the perfumed scent of shampoo. I rolled around in the dirt alongside her just for the joy of it. Heck, at this point, my state of cleanliness was so far gone that I had nothing left to lose. We spent several minutes on our backs with our feet in the air, wiggling back and forth like earthworms, making silly sounds and having a generally happy bonding experience.

Finally, we each sneezed like crazy, jumped to our feet, then lay down together side-by-side, panting and surveying our domain.

I told her everything that had happened to me that day. She was both horrified and fascinated. However, I didn't tell her about the private conversation Josh and I had, or that he held me and sobbed, because I didn't want to betray his confidence. I did tell her he had a gentle heart and asked her not to hold the unfortunate events of the day against him and his wife. I told her that Val had come to me and said I was much more than just a pretty face.

Maddie shrugged. *I've always known that about you.*

Really? Imagine that.

Thanks for taking such good care of my ranch, she said.

You're welcome. I did my best. I smiled at her. *And I have a whole new respect for you too.*

Josh's truck rumbled up and parked. He got out, walked over, and sat down between us. For a time, we all just silently drank in the beauty of Heavenly Acres Ranch.

Finally, he said to Maddie, "Lookin' forward to working with you."

Stay out of my way, let me do my job, and we'll get along just fine, she replied.

He laid his hand on my back. "I'm real proud to have known you, darlin'. Someday I'm gonna have another baby, and then there'll be grandbabies, and I'll still be telling tales about you."

Of course he would. I was the stuff of which legends

were made. Always had been, always will be.

He leaned over to smile at me, and I kissed him right on the lips. So, he kissed me on my nose. If he hadn't been married, and if he had been a dog, we might have had an interesting future together.

"Your folks want to clean you up and get you home, so it's time to go back now," he said.

I was ready. And since I had made my public statement of disgruntledness, I was eager to greet my humans like a happy dog should.

*   *   *

I kissed Angelina, I kissed Molly, and I even kissed Jessie, which was weird because she wasn't part of our pack—but I was just so grateful to be back with my people. I wiggled my butt joyfully and let out an inadvertent squeal of delight.

Cheyenne and Angelina gave me a bath with perfumed shampoo, dried and brushed my hair, and put a pretty pink bow on my head. They gave me a big bowl of my organic turkey and sweet potato, apple, and cranberry kibble, and an entire bottle of my special spring water.

Finally, Levi had a special gift for me from Val. Val had given it to Maddie last Christmas, but the preacher decided Val would want me to have it now. It was a blue denim neck scarf that was embroidered with the words MORDE DIEM.

"It's the cattle dog credo," Levi explained as he tied it around my neck. "It means, BITE THE DAY."

I had earned it, I deserved it, and I planned to wear it with pride.

*   *   *

To learn more about Talisman and her people, please read
the RED HOT series of comic novels:

www.RedHotNovels.com

TALISMAN AND MADDIE

The character of Talisman is based my own late Aussie, Kolbe. Maddie is based on her daughter, Maddie, who was a member of the Coakley family of Fort Collins, Colorado. The main difference between Kolbe and Maddie, was that Kolbe was a pampered show dog, while Maddie was one tough cookie.

Kolbe was just like Talisman: bottled water, organic kibble, massage therapist, pet psychic, and all. Seriously. (Well, I never did paint her toenails.) Like Talisman, Kolbe had enormous compassion and nobility.

Maddie was a delightful bitch-with-attitude who took on coyotes, hated to be groomed, and loved to herd anything and everything. She was fearless, tough, and lived for adventure. Maddie climbed mountains, fell off them, and survived.

Kolbe passed away in 2002 and Maddie passed away in 2010. They are together now, and the Coakleys and I hope the angels in charge of The Rainbow Bridge don't get the two of them confused. Remember guys, Kolbe expects to rest on that fluffy cloud and be fed treats. Maddie, on the other hand, will herd you and likely fall off one of those clouds while doing so. Just have a nice, soft lake for her to fall into like you provided that time she fell off the mountain.

To see photos of Kolbe and Maddie, and the other animals featured in Devin's novels, please visit "The Dogs and Cats" page on Devin's Website:
www.DevinWrites.com

ACKNOWLEDGMENTS

First off, I have to thank Karen Youmans for the *awesome* title.

For assistance with research, special thanks go out to Amy Bradley, Anne Jespersen, Terry Martin of Slash V Australian Shepherds, and Dave Farmer of Farmer Stockdogs.

For editing, I'd be lost without my friends and beta readers, Nicole Riviezzo and Julie Campbell.

My highly intelligent, wildly creative, and incredibly sexy writers' groups were amazing. The members of my critique groups contributed so much to this project that I can't begin to express my gratitude. For generously offering brilliant ideas that found their way into these pages, I especially want to thank Tammy Crosby and Austin Griffith. My online writers' group may be found at **forum.devinwrites.com** and we invite others to join us. We are a diverse community of writers, readers, artists, and animal-lovers.

Then there are my oh-so-special animal-loving Facebook friends who share so much with me. I couldn't do what I do without you guys! Join us on Facebook at:

www.facebook.com/devin.obranagan

THE RED HOT NOVELS

Red Hot Property is the first in a series of seriocomic novels chronicling the adventures of Molly O'Malley, a plucky rookie real estate agent who is learning to swim with the sharks at the town's most cutthroat agency. A former cocktail waitress, Molly uses her street savvy to avoid being eaten alive by vindictive office staff, neurotic colleagues, crazy clients, and an abundance of sexy men. A hilarious tale of a woman trying to become more than she believes possible, and discovering herself in the process.

In the second novel in the series, *Red Hot Liberty,* Molly O'Malley's new client, Liberty True, is a tin-foil-hat-wearing, conspiracy-theory-believing, rebel patriot who invites Molly to a different kind of tea party and drags her, kicking and screaming, into the revolution. Soon, Homeland Security is tailing Molly, and she is receiving death threats. Further complicating Molly's life is a rebellious daughter and a dog with romantic problems. A sassy tale about a woman on the verge of losing everything, who undertakes a quest to slay the dragon of fear and become her own hero.

Making a special guest appearance in *Red Hot Liberty* is Ch Caitland Isle Take A Chance, the first Australian Shepherd to win Best In Show at Crufts, the largest and most prestigious international dog show. Chance appears as Talisman's forbidden love. Also featured in *The Red Hot Novels* are real-life animals whose people entered raffles the author held to benefit the rescue organization Best Friends Animal Society.

WHAT THE CRITICS SAY

"*Red Hot Property* is sassy and simply entertaining..."
-*Women Writers Worldwide*

"A well-written and entertaining novel that will remind readers of Janet Evanovich's wildly successful Stephanie Plum novels." -*ForeWord Magazine*

"...a witty light read, loaded with vivid unforgettable characters who are sharply drawn and universally identifiable. Hilarious!" -*The Lyons Recorder*

"Captivating!" -*Boulder Women's Magazine*

"Devin O'Branagan's artful blending of humor, mystery and a delightful canine character make this a smooth, polished and absorbing read." -Judith Trustone, Author of *The Cats' Secret Guide to Living with Humans*

"O'Branagan has skill at developing characters and suspense." –*Rocky Mountain News*

www.RedHotNovels.com

ABOUT THE AUTHOR

Bestselling author Devin O'Branagan writes comic chick lit, canine chick lit, paranormal thrillers, urban fantasy, and a humor column for *TAILS Magazine*. Devin is a member of the Dog Writers Association of America, and she uses her writing projects to support animal rescue.

Visit her website at **www.DevinWrites.com**

10605609R0

Made in the USA
Lexington, KY
02 September 2011